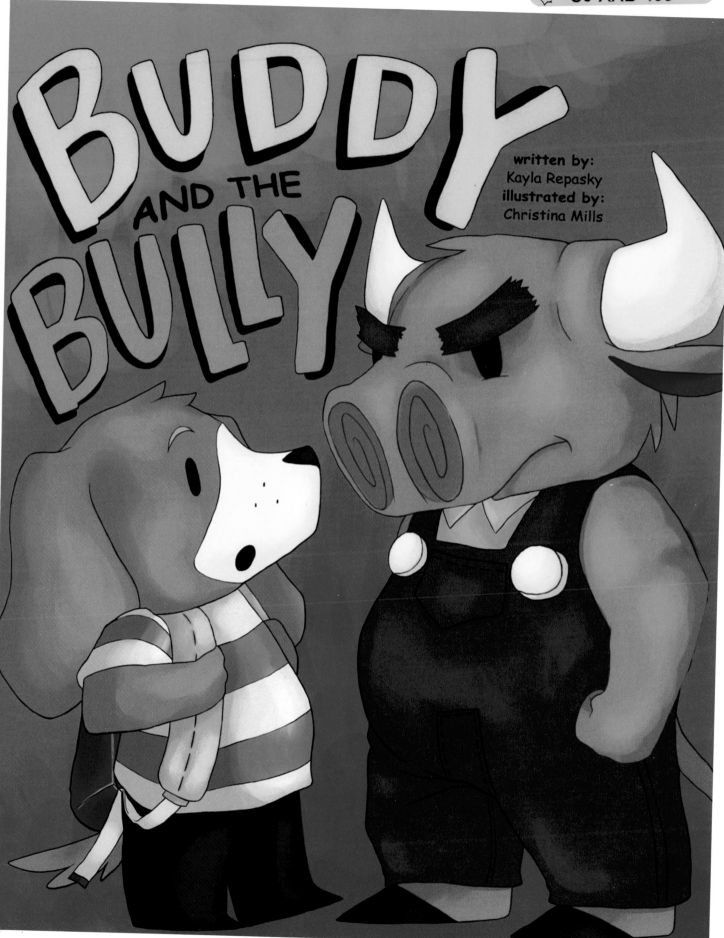

BUDDY
AND THE
BULLY

written by:
Kayla Repasky
illustrated by:
Christina Mills

Written by: Kayla Repasky
Illustrated by: Christina Mills

Once there was a dog named
BUDDY

Buddy loved to
play catch,
scratch his ears,
and roll in the
grass.

But most of all, Buddy loved school.
He loved to learn as much as he could
and play with all of his friends at school.

Everyone loved to play together.
Freddy the Frog, Ralph the Rabbit,
Maisy the Mouse, and Buddy.
They were the best of friends!

They would play together everyday,
while Billy the Bull would watch in anger.
He did not like to see Buddy and his
friends having fun.

Billy began to say mean things to Buddy. "You're not very good at playing catch," he would say. "No one likes you. You're not very smart."

Billy started to say these unkind words to Buddy everyday. He said them so often that he started to make Buddy feel very sad.

Buddy began to believe Billy.

He stopped playing catch with his friends, and he began to sit by himself at playtime.

Freddy, Ralph, and Maisy started to notice Buddy becoming sad and wanting to be by himself. So Ralph asked Buddy, "What's wrong?"

"Billy says that no one likes me and that I'm not very good at playing catch," he said as he began to cry.

"That's not true!"
replied his friends.

They began to think of
what they could do to help
Buddy.

"I have an idea." said Maisy.

"Let's tell Mrs. Gretel, our teacher!"

Freddy exclaimed, "Great idea!" So, that is what they did.

Mrs. Gretel was very happy that Buddy's friends came to her. She approached Billy and asked him, "Why are you saying such unkind things to Buddy?"

Billy replied, "I am different than everyone else. I am much bigger, and Buddy and his friends never invited me to play with them."

Mrs. Gretel smiled at Billy and said, "Just because you feel left out does not make it okay to be unkind to others."

She then looked at the group and said, "Have you ever asked Billy to play with you?"

Buddy thought about it and said, "I don't think we have ever asked Billy to play with us."

Mrs. Gretel smiled and said to the class,
"It is important to show kindness to everyone, even if
they are different than you."

"We would love for you to come and play with us," said Buddy.

"Yea!" added Maisy, "You can be on my team and help me. I am too small to catch sometimes."

Billy was so happy that he was invited to play catch! Billy gave Buddy a hug, and said, "I'm sorry for making you sad."

Buddy replied, "And I'm sorry for not asking you to play with us."

Buddy, Billy, Freddy, Ralph, and Maisy
became the best of friends and played
together everyday at recess.
They always remembered to be kind to
each other!

Here are a few discussion questions to assist you in reviewing the story with children.

1. How do you think Buddy felt when Billy the Bull was saying hurtful things towards him?

2. How did it make his friends feel?

3. What did Buddy's friends do to help Buddy?

4. How did Buddy and his friends show Billy the Bull kindness?

5. Why do you think Billy the Bull didn't like to see his friends have fun?

6. Why did Buddy sit alone?

7. Can you think of a time you felt left out or sad? What did you do?

8. If you are being bullied, or you see someone being bullied, what do you think you should do?

9. What does this story remind you of?

10. What are some ways that you can show kindness?

For more resources, visit thinkfirstamerica.com.